MOOMIN
Brilliantly Busy
Colouring Book

This book is coloured in by

_____

Write your name here!

PUFFIN

It is morning in the Moominhouse, and the Moomin

family are sitting down to breakfast.

Good morning, Moomintroll. What would you like to eat?

Outside the sun is shining,
and there's lots of gardening to do.

What beautiful flowers, Moominmamma. Don't forget to water them.

Pee-hoo! At last it's time
to go down to the beach.

Hurry up, Snorkmaiden! Don't get left behind!

The Moomins are very good swimmers.
They love diving and playing in the waves.

One, two, three . . .

Jump, Moominpappa!

It's always fun to go out in a boat.

Happy fishing, Moomins!

What a busy morning!
Now it's nearly time for lunch.

Mmm . . . What are you cooking on the campfire, Moomintroll?

Everyone is enjoying their picnic in the shade of the trees.

The sun has started to set, and it's almost time to go home. Who will get there first?

Have you had a lovely day, Snorkmaiden?

Back in the Moominhouse,
    there are more things to do . . .

Ooh . . . What are you knitting, Moominmamma?

... and there's a picture to finish!

What colour will your flowers be, Snorkmaiden?

It's very nearly bedtime, but first
the Moomins settle down for a story.

What's in the newspaper today, Moominpappa?

Now the moon shines high in the sky. The busy day is done and it's time to sleep.

Sweet dreams, Moomintroll.